Frankie

ISBN 978-1-0980-9087-6 (paperback)
ISBN 978-1-0980-9086-9 (digital)

Christian Faith Publishing, Inc.
832 Park Avenue
Meadville, PA 16335
www.christianfaithpublishing.com

Printed in the United States of America

Frankie

Theresa Richards

It was Monday morning again, and the Reynolds' household anxiously rushed through their Monday morning chores.

"Frances, breakfast is ready. Hurry or you'll be late for school!" shouted Mrs. Reynolds. "And you'd better bring along a sweater, you can never tell about this Spring Air."

"Okay, Mom," came the reply from the top of the stairs, and running down the staircase came a slender, young girl of eleven. She was rather tall for her age, almost too tall. Her hair was a light brown, the color of an almond, and hung long and straight, almost obstructing her vision.

"Frances, did you wash your hands and brush your teeth before breakfast?"

"Don't hound the girl, Martha," replied Mr. Reynolds as he read his morning paper over his coffee despite the protests of Mrs. Reynolds.

"Finish up your breakfast and run along now, Fran. You don't want to be late for school again, do you?" Mrs. Reynolds drew her daughter close to her as she kissed her goodbye.

Frances felt the warmth of her mother's closeness and the beating of her heart.

The door slammed, and another Monday morning began for Fran as she walked the two blocks to school.

"Hey, Fran!" shouted a familiar voice from behind, "I'll walk to school with you."

"Okay, Linda, but we have to walk quickly. If I'm late again today, my mom will have a canary!"

"Yeah, me too. I've been late three times this week, and if old Pussyfoot finds out about it, I know he'll make trouble."

Mr. McHugh was new at the Hetton school. The kids at school call him Pussyfoot because of the way he would sneak up and down the halls in his Hush Puppies.

"Hey, Frances, I'm going to buy a hero at your father's place today. Will you be there?"

"Sure, Linda, I'm always there. I go there for lunch every day and help out with the customers."

The Reynolds family owned a grocery store only a block from the school. It was a favorite place for Fran's friends to go for lunch.

"Okay, Fran, see you later."

Fran quickly entered her classroom, hung up her sweater, and proceeded to her desk. She sighed as she glanced at the clock. The bell rang almost immediately, and Mrs. Silver began her role call. Mrs. Silver never smiled. She was a tall woman, about fifty years of age with graying hair. Her face depicted not the slightest expression of kindness or compassion. Her dress was buttoned high at the neck, and she wore lace shoes and heavy stockings.

"Frances!" shouted Mrs. Silver. "Why don't you answer when I call your name? I was about to mark you absent."

"Excuse me, ma'am. I didn't hear you." Her voice trembled.

"From now on, you come to order and stop your daydreaming!"

"Yes, ma'am."

Fran didn't know why, but suddenly, she felt herself trembling all over. Mrs. Silver's voice vibrated in her head.

She felt the stares of ridiculing eyes surrounding her and absorbing her like a vacuum. Her temples pounded, and her cheeks turned the color of beets. Two girls giggled in the back row.

They're whispering there in the back row, she thought. *They're talking about me.*

The morning seemed like it would never end, and after a busy morning of English, History and Math, the afternoon lunch bell finally rang, and with it, for Fran, came a relaxation of tension and anxiety. She jumped from her seat, hurriedly fastened her sweater, and started down the two flights and into the street. She walked the one block to her father's grocery store, where she quickly ate her lunch and took her place behind the counter.

Then she noticed two boys walk in. She recognized them. They were both eighth grade students.

"How much are the eggs, Fran?"

"Two dollars a dozen."

"We need three dozen. Here's a dollar. I'll have to owe you the rest."

"Well, I don't know. I'll have to ask…"

"Oh, come on. I'll give you the rest tomorrow."

"Well, I guess I could trust you. Okay."

Frances wondered at the strange purchase made by the two boys.

"Oh well," she sighed as she walked slowly to the backroom to get her sweater.

It was twelve thirty. She had fifteen minutes before the first bell rang. As she walked along the familiar path toward the red school house, the thought of the two boys puzzled her and repeatedly entered her mind.

She leaned against the fence for a few minutes until she decided to go in a little early. As she was about to enter her classroom, she suddenly detected a strange but familiar odor. It reminded her of the store, of groceries, of *eggs*! Her eyes crawled up the wall like a caterpillar. Then she knew why the eggs were bought.

There, along the entire length of the corridor walls, over the bulletin boards and posters were eggs and more eggs. Egg shells were cracked on the floor; some of the shells were stuck on the walls where the egg yolks held them in a sticky mess. Her heart leaped! She thought it would leap right out of her chest!

It was me, she repeated to herself over and over again. *I sold them the eggs. I should've known they would do something like this. If I tell on them, they'll know who told. They'll get me if I tell, I know they will.*

She raced down the hall almost panic-stricken with fear. She wanted to speak to someone and share her problem with someone. She noticed Linda walking down the corridor from the opposite direction.

"Why, Fran, what's the matter with you?" asked Linda.

"You mean you don't know, Linda? Didn't you see the corridor walls? There are eggs thrown all over the walls!"

"What? But who did it?"

"Oh, Linda, if Mr. McHugh finds out who did it, somebody's gonna get expelled, I know."

"Well, what are you so upset about? You had nothing to do with it, Fran."

"Oh yes, I did, Linda." Fran explained her situation to her friend, not leaving out one minor detail.

"Gee, Fran, what are you gonna do?" said Linda after hearing Fran's story.

"That's just it, Linda, I don't know. If my parents find out about me knowing who threw the eggs, they'll make me tell. And if I do tell, the kids will get me for it, I know."

"Gee, Fran, you really have a problem."

Classes were called off that afternoon in order for the janitors to clean up. Mr. McHugh called a special assembly for the entire school.

"I guess you know why I called you here this afternoon," began Mr. McHugh.

"By now, you must have seen the corridor walls. I just want to let you know that I'm going to find out who was responsible for this disgraceful act! I promise I'll find out, and when I do, you all know what the result will be. Now I'm not going to keep the entire school here to be disciplined, but there's one last thing. If anyone knows anything about this or has any idea who may have been responsible, I want him or her to come to me privately. I promise I'll not reveal your identity."

Frances felt a strange sensation at the bottom of her throat. It felt like she swallowed a frog. Her heart pounded violently as if it would never stop again. She glanced to the side of the auditorium. They were there!

She knew where they usually sat. They turned and stared into her eyes.

"Frances, you haven't touched your dinner," said Mrs. Reynolds later that night.

"I'm just not hungry, Mom. Sorry."

14

"Now you know you have to eat, dear. It's not good for you not to. By the way, Fran, Linda's mother told me there was some trouble at the school today."

"What's that?" replied Mr. Reynolds.

"Well, John, it seems that some boys splattered the corridor walls with eggs."

"That's just terrible. These young kids nowadays. Why when I was a boy…"

"Now, John, we've heard all about your childhood days before."

"What I'm trying to say, Martha, is that it's not just the kids who are to blame, it's the parents too. A lot more of those kids would be caught and punished if the proper authorities were given information as to who were responsible. The trouble today is that the parents don't raise their children to be responsible citizens. Why if my Franny had seen anything…"

She couldn't take it anymore. She jumped up from the table and leaped up the stairs amid the astonished eyes of her parents. Tears gathered in her eyes.

They don't know me, she thought to herself. *I'm not who they think I am. I'm just no good, no good for anything.*

She sobbed unceasingly but quietly. She didn't want her parents to hear her. Falling on her bed, she hid her face under her pillow, sobbing continuously.

Responsible citizen, she repeated to herself. *What does that mean? To the kids at school, it means you're a tattletale. To your parents, it means you're a failure. Responsible citizen. Ha! I just want to be Fran Reynolds!*

The next day, Fran walked into her classroom and sat at her desk. She felt a little better. Even Mrs. Silver looked slightly human today. Between classes, Fran was her usual self. She talked with her friends about everything and nothing. The lunch bell rang, and as she was preparing to leave the classroom, she was jolted back into the reality of her problem by the faces of the two boys. She tried to tell them with her eyes that she would not tell. She tried to make them understand.

Fran was the last one out of the classroom that day, and as she approached the door, she saw Mr. McHugh standing there at the opposite end of the corridor. He stood tall and strong looking at her.

From her end of the hall, Fran stood small and weak. She thought he looked strange. He appeared supreme and confident. Maybe he knew all along and was waiting for her to come to him. Now he has come to her, to judge her. The corridor was quiet, almost solemn, as he finally approached her.

"Hello, Frances," he said with an air of compassion and kindness in his voice. "I'd like to speak with you in my office."

He knew! Now she was certain of it. *He knew all along. They all knew. Everyone knows about my father's grocery store.*

"Now, Frances, you know why you are here," began Mr. McHugh after they were seated in his office.

"Now, Fran," he repeated, "I want you to tell me to whom you sold the eggs."

"I don't know."

"Of course, you do. Don't be afraid, dear. I won't tell anyone you told me. You can trust me."

"I can't tell you," repeated Fran.

"Fran, you have an obligation…"

"Please, please!" cried Fran. "I want to go home, just let me go home. Please, Mr. McHugh!"

They were both silent for what seemed like an eternity.

Finally, Mr. McHugh uttered, "Okay, Fran, I won't push you. I understand. You may leave. You can go now if you want."

Fran looked at his face. It was so depressed, so old. He looked defeated. She rose from her chair, turned, and walked slowly out of the office. She was free. She knew they wouldn't make her tell now. She should have felt happy, but she didn't, somehow. Halfway down the corridor, she stopped. Her heart pounded as she fought within herself. The handkerchief she held was wet and wrinkled from where she squeezed it between her trembling hands.

She wanted to walk away, but she knew she couldn't. All along she had fought against what she knew must be done in the end.

Turning around, she slowly walked back down the hall, opened the door to Mr. McHugh's office, and walked inside.

About the Author

Theresa Richards is the mother of two grown children, whom she calls her blessings. She strives every day to follow the teachings of her hero, Mother Teresa.

"I believe love begins at home. How can you give to the outside what you don't have on the inside?"

Ms. Richards is a strong animal advocate, having rescued three chihuahuas.

"I am their whole world. They literally jump for joy when I get home."

CPSIA information can be obtained
at www.ICGtesting.com
Printed in the USA
BVHW061034291121
622781BV00010B/479

9 781098 090876